The Lig

by

Dinah Dillman Kaufman

cover illustration by

Christopher Dillman

Avid Readers Publishing Group

Lakewood, California

This is a work of fiction. The opinions expressed in this manuscript are the opinions of the author(s) and do not represent the thoughts or opinions of thepublisher. The author(s) warrants and represents that he/she has the legal right to publish or owns all material in this book. If you find a discrepancy,contact the publisher at arpg@ericpatterson.name.

The Lighthouse

Cover by Christopher Parker Dillman

Avid Readers Publishing Group

http://www.avidreaderspg.com

ISBN-13: 978-1-935105-27-5

Printed in the United States

Dedication

This book is for my loving, supportive husband whose encouragement helped me write this story.

This book is for my son Seth who made our trip to Catalina a memorable one.

This book is for my father who showed me the light I needed to write and to my mother whose red flame has never burned out.

There was blood on the bottom stoop of the old Crawford lighthouse. The red sticky mess led to the top where there lay a horrendous sight: a corpse of a woman whom I presumed was very well off because she wore an expensive Chanel suit and had lovely manicured hands. I recognized the color as fire engine red because my mother wore the same.

My name is Rusty Parker. I am a photographer for the Crime Scene Investigation unit on the Isle of Cortez. I was put on this case when I received a call about a wealthy socialite, a Ms. Sylvia Crawford who had been brutally murdered. Next to arrive on the scene was Lt. Jack Levitt. "Parker," he said, "What do we have here?"

"I don't know sir, still checking things out," answered Rusty.

Lt. Levitt assured, "I will have my men secure the area's to keep the lookie loos at bay."

The body was still warm. The brutal attack must have happened a couple of hours prior to Rusty's arrival. The beautiful white suit was now covered in red. I took a picture of her body position and noted that she had lost a shoe. It had fallen down approximately 49 steps. I am a fan of Hitchcock and this seemed right up his alley. Ah, I spotted the shoe, behind a bougainvillea bush. I zoomed in a picture of what looked like to be a high-heeled Jimmy Choo. I give this lady kudos for her taste in fashion. I also noted a single white gardenia in her left hand.

I took pictures of all I saw before Lt. Levitt called the coroner and next of kin. "Do you see any entry wounds, Parker?" asked Lt. Levitt. He nodded permission for me to turn the body over on to its back. It was no longer a "Woman," just another corpse. There I noticed three puncture holes. One was in the upper back, one to the left lung and one to the right. I pondered the possibility that Sylvia Crawford had been murdered by a left-handed person due to the direction of the entry wounds. "What do you make of this Parker," he inquired. I kept my suspicions to myself until I was sure, taking note of the blood trail on the steps leading up to the body.

Lt. Levitt and I have worked on many cases

together. He called me Parker, "Don't like Rusty," he always joked.

"And I don't like my birth name of Evelyn, which means shining light, by the way. My dad had always called me Rusty since as long as I could remember," I felt I had to explain. "My dad told me he called me Rusty because of the color of my hair. The name kind of clicked, like the sound of a camera."

The next day, Lt. Levitt brought over to my cubicle, a file on Ms. Crawford. I was more than just a photographer; I was a member of a team. Our CSI unit was the only one on the Isle of Cortez. It was very easy to get around; walking was the norm in the town of Annabillow. Only the lighthouse looked out of place. While the Aztec-style town had new structures and had updated looks, the lighthouse remained out-dated, as did the immense Spanish- style dwelling of the Crawfords. Sylvia Crawford herself was timeless.

I went on to read about Ms. Crawford. She'd been married to Charles Morgan and had two children, two boys. There was a family picture; I looked over. Happier days, I imagined. They were down by the Marina. I made a note of the names and date of the photograph in my black book.

I recognized Sylvia right away. Besides a fake smile, she wore a fancy sailing outfit. I noted the black pearl necklace, probably Tahitian, I imagined. It looked familiar from those travel books of my dad's. Next to her was Charles, wearing that same artificial smirk. He had his hand in one pocket and the other around Sylvia. He looked like quite the captain in his navy blazer and white slacks. Only the boys looked unhappy, as if uncomfortable to be seen with their "phony-baloney" parents. I noted their names; Skyler and River. In the photo they looked to be 8.

The photo was dated 1986. That made the boys about 21. I made a note to ask Charles why Sylvia still went by Crawford instead of Morgan, Skyler and River too. "Rusty, did you find something of interest?" my associate, Lauren Matthews asked as she entered my turf. Lauren is a neat nik, I am not. I cleared off a chair stacked with files for her to sit down.

"For someone who is good at organizing crime photos, you would think you could organize your desk," she joked. Lauren is about my age, 42. She started at the same time as I did, about three years ago as a coroner. Lt. Levitt always jested, "I hired you Parker for your brains, and Lauren for her good looks." Yes, I had to admit that Lauren was a pretty blonde. She had soulful brown eyes. She was nice and well liked by all. Not that I wasn't easy on the eyes. My 5'6 frame is pear shaped. My blue eyes accentuate my auburn hair.

I had inherited my Nana Moore's hips. I had to be careful with my diet. Living with just my dad, made it hard at times. He rarely left his chair. Ever since my mom died five years ago, he has been determined to not leave the roost. My mom was quite the beauty, back in her heyday. I got my hair color from my dad, but inherited my mom's eyes. Her hair was as black as night, her eyes as blue as the sea. Her name was Cordelia, which meant "Protector of the Sea" or so she often bragged. I would like to think she was my special guardian, my guiding light.

I liked to spin; it kept both my mind and spirit clear of any obstacles. My dad didn't exercise. At 78, he was slowing down a bit. "Rusty, you are just as nagging as your mom." He complained every time I asked him to join me.

My dad is my inspiration. Daniel Lofton Parker was an engineer on the island. He designed many of the landmarks, including the Crawford lighthouse. He now was retired, living with a nagging daughter. "It's because I care for you dad, that I hope to motivate you," I often explained.

My mom was a swimmer. She loved the water, ever since she was little. She made sure I had lessons when I was young. After throwing me into the lake at 2 and watching me struggle, she yelled, "Now swim, Evelyn. Don't be so lazy." I had no choice but to oblige. It was either sink or swim. I chose the latter. Mom had an opportunity to turn pro, but had me instead. I have an article about the last lap of "Cordelia Parker" stating her fame, her rise to the top, her chance to turn pro and her decision to quit at the peak of her career. I often asked her why she stopped and she explained, "I wanted a child, a beautiful girl, like you Evelyn." She didn't call me Rusty. It was just between my dad and me.

My cubicle seemed popular this morning. In walked Gavin Cain as Lauren left asking me to join her to spin this weekend. I told her yes. "Can I come too?" Gavin joked. I shrugged, as I replied, "no" adding, "if you come Gavin, we wouldn't be able to gossip about you." Gavin was the team's forensic specialist and had a big ego. He stomped off in a huff, tossing his blond locks. Gavin had been with the squad for a long time and was hoping for a transfer. He complained about how he didn't like the smells of the sea and preferred his ranch in Texas. Gavin often bragged that his great grandmother Lizzie Mae

Cain had been the sheriff of San Antonio. He came to the Isle of Cortez because of this job, though I think even Texas, wasn't grand enough for the almighty Cain.

The four of us, including Lt. Levitt, made a fantastic foursome. The four Musketeers, I often joked. So here we were once again trying to put pieces together of a rather perplexing puzzle.

The murder of Sylvia Crawford made news quickly. Town gossip spread like the plague. I went back to the site as I saw vultures circling. In the mist of the chaos was a reporter from the Annabillow ANECDOTE. He saw me. "Parker," he rushed right over. I looked Stan Gertz directly in the eye and said, "No comment."

"Aw, come on Parker," he taunted.

"First of all, I am not Parker to anyone outside my clan. And second, if you must talk to me Stan, call me Rusty," I calmly explained.

"Ok, Rusty. What's the scoop?" asked Stan. I leaned over and whispered in a low sexy voice, "No comment." I left him standing in the dust of my fast moving pace.

InsidetheCSIbuilding,Laurenwasbusyexamining

Sylvia Crawford's cadaver. She carefully placed gloves on her manicured appendages while balancing her glasses on her nose, not wanting to miss the tiniest blemish. Sylvia was in great form, Lauren thought, studying the different surgeries she had. A nip here and a tuck there. With her money, Sylvia could afford the moon and the stars.

Lauren made a note of the markings on Sylvia's back. Someone had used a sharp blunt instrument to pierce a well-toned back three times. Lauren being a novice sailor shared her findings with Lt. Levitt as he entered the room with Rusty stating, "If you connected all three points, they could make a sail, like on a ship." Rusty shared her thoughts about the possibility of a left-handed killer and asked about the markings on the victim's neck as she took a picture, observing, "It looks like someone yanked off a piece of jewelry."

"Any prints, Mathews?" Lt. Levitt inquired. As Lauren dusted around the neck, she found a print.

Next morning, Charles Morgan received a message from Lt. Levitt. He had been hard to reach ever since the deceased was discovered. It turned out that Charles had made that urgent call after stumbling upon his spouse. Within the hour, he welcomed Lt. Levitt and his squad to his humble abode. "Lt, it's indeed a pleasure," Charles said as he extended his left hand to meet Lt. Levitt's right. Lt. Levitt introduced his team, "This is my crew, Parker, Matthews and Cain." Charles was alongside his boys. Again, introductions were made.

"I am sorry for your loss. May I have a look around?" Rusty asked with camera in hand. "Yes, help yourself but be careful with the artifacts," Charles said eyeing Gavin as he was about to plod on the family pet. Gavin quickly moved. "This is Ronrico, a Maltese," Charles began to explain. I took a picture, had to. The dog was dressed in a sailor outfit.

Besides Charles and his less than cordial sons, there was a staff to greet us. Anges Reeves introduced himself as the butler. Ms. Dorcas Sanders was Sylvia's personal attendant. Bertha Brown was the cook, Gretchen Anderson was the housemaid and there was a chauffeur that just went by Winston. I looked them over with a keen eye. Anges looked to be about 60 and worked for the family for about 25 years. He extended a firm left-handed handshake. Ms. Sanders was pretty, I thought, maybe 19? And she had a nice curtsey and a welcoming hello. For my own curiosity, I questioned her first name. She explained her folks were fans of Shakespeare and she was born on what was believed to be his birthday, April 18th. The name Dorcas was from his play, "A Winter's Tale."

Bertha was what I imagined a cook would look like, pleasantly plump with a warm smile. Gretchen looked like a scared mouse, like she was hiding something, perhaps a piece of cheese. She didn't even look me straight in the eye, just stared at the floor. I then heard a loud coughing sound. Gretchen quickly looked to Anges who eyed her sternly. She obediently curtseyed, like a trained rodent. Then there was Winston. I was later told he had been with the Crawfords the longest, about 30 years. He was in charge of caring for the Crawfords six cars. The Bentley was a personal favorite of his. After the introductions, they all scampered off to work, except Anges, who asked, "Will there be anything else?"

"No, but stay close in case we have further questions," said Lt. Levitt.

What a house. Living in a modest condo by the docks seemed dull by comparison, as I gazed at the massive structure before me. Finally the privilege was granted to enter. I felt I was trespassing. "No flash photography, Ms. Parker," Anges ordered.

"These tapestries and oil paintings are very old. The flash would ruin the colors." I quickly turned my flash off. The Cathedral ceilings were the first to catch my eye. Anges started the tour downstairs. In the kitchen were Bertha and her assistant. Her tag read "Heather." The oven smelled good. I asked what they were baking.

"Master River and Master Skyler cherish my Chocolate Chip cookies," Bertha proudly proclaimed. I admit they looked yummy but I was too timid to ask for one.

The kitchen was a dream. It had a walk-in storage closet, piled to the brim with all the necessities. A center island with copper pots and pans strewn from above. This room led to the dining room where we found Charles. "This was Sylvia's favorite room, Ms. Parker. It is where we all dined together as a family," explained Charles. As a family, I wondered what he meant by that? I noticed the dining table seated twelve. The finest china was properly placed.

My team and I continued the tour which felt like a museum guided journey. Off the kitchen was the servant's quarters. I made a note of the size of each room. Bertha and Heather shared a room, as did Anges and Winston. Dorcas and Gretchen's room was upstairs close to Sylvia's room. Charles told us that he had his own room downstairs. He jested that he preferred it that way so he could raid the refrigerator if he felt a need. Charles added that both Skyler and River had a separate room upstairs close to their mother's, if Sylvia had a need for her sons.

We walked out the back door onto a glorious garden. I noticed the roses. "Sylvia prided herself on her roses," Charles remarked, adding, "Just Joey was her favorite." There was a gardener pruning back a bougainvillea bush. Charles introduced him as Phuong Nugyen, from Vietnam. Anges approached with a note in his hand. "My apologies, sir," he said as he handed Charles the note. "Will you please excuse me, Ms. Parker? I need to tend to this." I snapped more pictures of the garden. It was so beautiful. My mom would have loved the colors and smells. I walked to the atrium and sat down taking in all the quiet beauty until it was loudly disturbed.

The clamor and commotion belonged to a neighbor who had shown up unexpectedly. "This is George Radcliff," announced Charles. George's entrance was extremely unsettling because my ideal tranquility was ruined. "Are you with the press?" George inquired.

"No, I am Rusty Parker. I am with the CSI division." I looked at Charles to come to my aid.

"CSI?" George began, adding," That's intriguing." Charles explained, "She and her team are here about Sylvia's murder." The rosy color in George's face turned white. He stared at us expressionless.

Charles asked, "Didn't you know? It's been all over the news."

"I have been out of town, old chap. Just got back today," explained George.

I am usually good at reading people's faces though I couldn't make out George's. He was very distinguished looking, even down to the monocle on the left eye. He looked to be the same age as Charles. He donned an evening jacket with a single white gardenia in the lapel and nice slacks. He was rather dressed up for a morning call. I had to ask, "Mr. Radcliff, where did you return from?"

"My, what pretty hair color you have, Ms. Parker. What shade is it?" he responded, evading my question.

I answered, "My own." I again asked about his whereabouts.

"Ms. Parker, I travel all over the world. I don't see how it is any of your business where I vacation. I find your tone to be tiresome and trivial." And off he sauntered like a proud peacock leaving me in his polluted air.

I noticed George was walking towards the docks. I decided to follow him. He began talking to a steward as he boarded a fancy looking yacht. I made a mental note of the name on the ships stern, "Blue Angel" and phoned Lauren.

Back at the CSI lab, Lauren was busy analyzing the victim and by using special tape, lifted a print from her neck. There must have been a necklace Lauren decided because of the severity of the dents in her flesh, as if the killer had ripped off a piece of jewelry. The slide Lauren used to find a print was placed on the tray of her telescope. Lauren quickly wrote down her findings. She discovered some nail fibers that might have possible DNA. Lauren spoke to Rusty on her headset. "I'm on my way to talk to Lt. Levitt. Where are you, Rusty?"

"I am by the docks, by a yacht rented by George

Radcliff," Rusty answered.

"Is it a sail boat?" Lauren wondered. Lauren recalled the markings on Sylvia's back that looked like a sail. Lauren felt she had probable cause as she said, "I'll try to get a warrant from Commissioner Dean Bedford to search Mr. Radcliff's yacht. Sometimes we need to go to a higher rank to move things along quicker."

Saturday found Lauren and me in our spin class. We were pedaling as fast as our feet could possibly move, listening to our instructor, Jane enthusiastically shout for us to turn the knob and add a little resistance. "Everyone up!" she hollered as she had everyone's adrenaline up and running. After the class, Lauren and I went our separate ways. While I live with my dad, Lauren lived alone in a one-bedroom apartment on Pine Avenue. "See you Monday," she chirped as she glided into her car and drove to an empty nest.

Lauren had been married before, to a Roark Neilson. She never talked about it, only to say it had been a mistake. Lauren recently bought a Calico cat, to fill the void, she claimed. She named him T-Bear and he gave the best cat hugs. "Who needs a man to make me feel needed and happy when I have you my pet," as they both purred cheerfully. The phone by her bed rang. She wasn't expecting a call. "Hello," she said hoping it was a man's voice, perhaps Roark's? Maybe he realized his big mistake and wanted her back. "Hello," replied the voice. It was Gavin's.

Gavin Cain knew he was gorgeous. He treasured his chiseled looks and was always surprised when Lauren turned down his dinner invitations. Being from Texas, Gavin had a slight accent, a particular stammer that Lauren admitted to herself was cute. "Gavin, is there a problem with work?" Lauren asked. It was a weekend though Gavin often worked overtime.

"No. Just wanted to hear your sweet voice, Lauren," Gavin answered. Even though he was good looking, he was lonely. Gavin could have any girl at any time but his heart belonged to Lauren. "I am sorry Gavin, but I need to go. See you at work, ok?" Lauren tried to sound reassuring. "Ok," Gavin replied and hung up to drive to his home.

Gavin lived in a one-bedroom apartment on Oak Drive. He had never been in a serious relationship. His black phone rang very seldom and his answering machine had few messages of value. As he entered his hollow home, he thought about calling Lauren again. He reached for the extension and noticed a photo on the kitchen counter-top of him, Rusty and Lauren. Seeing the picture made Gavin smile. Instead of calling Lauren, he dialed Rusty.

Living with her dad had good points and bad. Rusty became her dad's caretaker. She liked to take care of him but she missed her mom, now even more because today was the anniversary of her death. The coroner at the time listed her death as "Accidental drowning," though Rusty had her doubts. Her mom's ashes were sprinkled in the water during a private ceremony.

In honor of her mom, Rusty and her dad lit a candle and said a small prayer. Even though time had passed, it was still hard on both of them. "You need to find a nice man and settle down, Rusty. You shouldn't have to care for an old man like me," Rusty's dad said.

"Old? Dad you are in your prime. I enjoy looking after you. Mom would like it that way. Besides, there is no man as charming as you, dad," exclaimed Rusty.

Daniel Parker had a good reputation around town. His blue prints and structures were well known and at one time kept him busy. He met Cordelia Ann Roberts on a warm Sunday afternoon at Back Bay Beach about forty-five years ago. She was frolicking about in the waves and he was instantly smitten by her striking beauty. He was bold enough to ask her to dine with him. She was eager enough to except. The rest is personal, though I can report that they eloped shortly after. My mom took on Parker as her last name. My dad often teased her about her new initials, C.A.R.P jesting she was like a fish in and out of the water. I came along two years later in 1965. My dad not only talked about his great love, his wife, but of his other accomplishment, the Crawford Lighthouse. He was most proud of that, it was his claim to fame. The lighthouse was put on the map as the most wondrous sight to see in Annabillow. Now the sight was famous for a murder.

Rusty let the machine pick up the ringing telephone. She didn't want to talk to anyone. She listened to the message from Gavin, who needed a friend. He forgot what this day was to Rusty. Daniel was sitting in his favorite chair, clicker in hand watching the old movie station along with his number one girl. He and Rusty had a common bond when it came to the films from the 1930's and 1940's. "Citizen Kane" was his favorite while "Gone with the Wind" was hers. Today in honor of her mom, they watched her favorite, "The Way We Were." The movie was made in 1973. Rusty would have been about 8.

Over at the station, Lt. Levitt was looking at the picture of River and Skyler Crawford. He noted from the back their age was marked as 8. He noticed from his file that the boys had the same birth date, April 14, 1987. They were twins. Lt. Levitt made arrangements to bring them in for questioning.

Lt. Levitt's clock struck 9:00 AM that next morning. Skyler was prompt after being summoned by telephone. "Welcome. Please have a seat Mr. Morgan," began Lt. Levitt.

"Thank you. We don't use Morgan. Our last name is Crawford. Please call me Skyler, Lt."

"Where is your brother, River?" asked Lt. Levitt. "He is always late. He will probably be late to his own funeral," Skyler jested.

Lt. Levitt looked at this young man with striking good looks and questioned, "Where does the name Skyler come from?"

"The sky" was his smart-alec reply. Just then River came in. He was three minutes late.

"Sorry, but I seem to be always late," he said, adding, "We were born three minutes apart."

Though they were twins, they looked nothing like each other. Skyler had the movie star looks and seemed confident; River looked disheveled and seemed shy.

"I have asked you here to talk about your mother and also to let you know how deeply sorry my team and I are about her death." Lt. Levitt began, adding, "I realize this is a hard time for you so I went ahead and released your mother's body to your father. He told me that there will be a private funeral for your mother and he didn't want you to be worrying about anything so he made all the arrangements."

Both Skyler and River were in shock. Skyler stated, "My mother wished to be cremated and her ashes thrown to the sea." River nodded and agreed. Skyler added, "It was a verbal understanding that we all knew and supported. My mother never mentioned other intentions and I am not privy to a Will or other arrangements."

River asked, "Did my dad have permission to take my mother's body? I thought this was a murder investigation. Don't you need her body to find out what happened and who did this to her?"

Lt. Levitt explained all his investigation findings to the boys and that Charles was listed as next of kin. Charles made all the necessary arrangements for Sylvia's remains. "I am sorry. Your mother was cremated and your father took her ashes home in an urn when he left the crematorium. Now, no disrespect to your mother, did she have any enemies? Who would want her dead?" asked Lt. Levitt. Both Skyler and River looked at each other and at the same time said, "Our father."

It was no secret that Skyler and River didn't like their father. They used their mother's surname of Crawford because she wanted it that way; it was to make her happy. They were mamma's boys through and through.

Sylvia Elaine Crawford was born into a rich family. Her father Braden had been a stockbroker and her mother Andrea, an acclaimed opera singer. Sylvia was spoiled being an only child. She longed for nothing. Sylvia and Charles now lived in the estate that she grew up in. Sylvia's parents wanted the house kept in the family. Braden and Andrea were afraid developers would build a house on their third lawn. So when her parents passed away, Sylvia took ownership of the property resting on two and half acres. It was built on top of a natural hot spring with views overlooking the ocean in Annabillow.

Sylvia spent most of her youth with a nanny.

She was home schooled having the best tutors money could buy. Braden and Andrea had a full household staff. Only two still remained in employment, Anges Reeves and Winston. The other staff was hired as needed.

Lt. Levitt thanked both River and Skyler for their honesty. They quickly left. Lt Levitt then summoned Charles Morgan by messenger. Lt. Levitt read that Charles Andrew Morgan came from a very humble beginning. His father had left a few days after he was born. Charles was raised by his mother, Dorothy, a schoolteacher. She also worked as a seamstress to make ends meet.

"It looks to me that Charles married into the Crawford family for their money," Lt. Levitt said to himself adding, "A possible motive for murder." It was the end of another dreary day. Hopefully, tomorrow's outlook would be brighter.

The following morning at 9:00 AM promptly, Charles strolled cheerfully into the police station. He had the look of a man who had just won the lottery, not of a man who had just lost his wife. His clothes were pressed and he was well groomed, down to the gardenia in his lapel.

"Lt. Levitt, how are you this fine day?" asked Charles.

"Please have a seat, Mr. Morgan," Lt. Levitt started.

"My friends call me Charles," was his reply.

"I have some questions Charles. For my curiosity, why did Sylvia use Crawford instead of Morgan as her last name?" Lt. Levitt inquired.

"It was her father's wish if she ever married, she would use his surname to keep the Crawford family legacy intact. The Crawfords were well known in this community, their name stood out, like that gigantic eyesore she grew up in," Charles answered.

"What about the lighthouse? Was it built at the same time as the house?" asked Lt. Levitt, adding, "It looked outdated, like it didn't belong there."

"The house itself has been changed over the years, to appease Sylvia. This latest venture was an Aztec style. Sylvia had a craving for an Indian flavor due to her art teacher's method of painting. Edwin Villa, her instructor, is Native American. Daniel Parker designed the lighthouse;

he would have the original prints. It is best to ask him about it because I've never gone near the lighthouse since it was constructed about ten years ago. It was built to be Sylvia's studio, her private oasis away from home. Sylvia loved the stars. She said she had a better view of them and felt closest to her mother at the very top. She could hear foghorns from passing ships there, she explained the tranquility of the sounds was her inspiration for painting; she loved the sea and was an expert sailor. Her mother was an opera singer, you see. Sylvia often said she could hear her mother's voice as if she was right there by her side every time she went into the lighthouse." Charles looked lost in the memory, holding back tears that were trying to escape his weeping eyes. Lt. Levitt thanked Charles for his candor. This case is getting more intriguing, Lt. Levitt thought.

The day of Sylvia's funeral was somber. The forecast called for light rain though it poured. Sylvia's cremated body was packed in an urn, held by Charles. Reverend Ivan Vogel performed the service at a private gravesite. Close friends and family were in attendance. I was surprised Charles had requested that Lt. Levitt and I be present. Charles approached, "Ms. Parker and Lt. Levitt, thank you for coming." He added, "Please have a seat. We will begin shortly."

Lt. Levitt and I took our cue. The services were about to begin. How private was this service supposed to be? I noticed my surroundings; it was a small cemetery that had the name "Crawford" on the front gate. This must be a family plot, I figured. I saw Sklyer and River sitting in the front row. River was in tears while Skyler just stared ahead. I was surprised to see Sylvia's personal maid, Dorcas, there because the other staff members were not. Dorcas saw me and came right over. "Ms. Parker, I am glad you came today," she said and hurried back to her seat. She would be here, I thought because she was Sylvia's personal attendant.

I recognized George Radcliff; he nodded to me as he cleaned his monocle with what looked like a woman's hanky. He came over to me to ask why I was there. "I was asked by Charles," was my quick reply adding, "I could ask you the same question Mr. Radcliff."

"Ms. Parker, I am a dear, dear friend of Charles and Sylvia. It's rather tragic what happened to her." The smell of his cologne made me sneeze. "Bless you good woman," George said as he handed me a handkerchief. I noticed the initials monogrammed were S.E.C. I assumed for Sylvia Elaine Crawford. I wondered where he got it from. "Just keep it Ms. Parker. Funerals can be a bit messy," he said. I thanked him and he found his seat.

Other faces were not as familiar in the crowd. Friends of Sylvia's I gathered. Charles was found seated next to an exquisite looking woman wearing an elegant hat, concealing her face. She was holding his hand. I assumed to comfort him in his hour of bereavement. Reverend Vogel opened his Bible and began his sermon. I watched Charles expression as the Reverend spoke. He didn't show any emotion. The Reverend ended, "With ashes to ashes and dust to dust." Sylvia was ash now since Charles had her cremated, not giving his sons a chance to see their mother one last time. There was no body for the family to mourn, to say their goodbyes. Charles took the urn to the family crypt followed by the Reverend, Skyler and River.

"Parker," Lt. Levitt began. "I will see you back at the station."

"Ok, sir," I said adding, "I want to have a look around." As Lt. Levitt left, I noticed Stan Gertz. "I didn't realize the media was invited, Stan," I said.

"I didn't realize that the CSI was as well," he

said in jest adding, "Do you have a take on this investigation?"

"Stan, this is a funeral. Show some respect. Leave the family alone today. Where is your heart Stan?" I asked. Stan Gertz never let on to anyone that his heart belonged to Rusty.

Stan had known Rusty since their sandbox days in Kindergarten. While the other girls were playing with dolls, Rusty preferred the mud and insects that the boys were into. Ladybugs were her favorite. Rusty was a bit of a tomboy and enjoyed getting dirty. She hit Stan in the eye when he tried to innocently kiss her. From that moment on, Stan was smitten.

"Sorry Rusty, you're right." Stan said and left quickly to not show any emotion. The rain that fell during the funeral remarkably lifted the next day. Birds could be heard chirping. It was the end of spring. Soon it would be tourist time in Annabillow. Vacationers who sailed there often slept on their boats or in the local hotel. They came to this town to relax.

Charles Morgan couldn't relax. He was anxiously awaiting the reading of Sylvia's Will. Their family attorney called for a meeting within weeks after the funeral. Irving Kaplan summoned the family and those concerned by messenger to meet in his law office. I was notified to represent the CSI. I was the only one from our team. Stan was there to represent the media since Sylvia was well known within the community.

We all sat down around what seemed a triangle-shaped table. Why was that shape in my head? Irving was at the top, Charles to his left, leaving a seat unoccupied by him. Skyler and River were to the right. Anges Reeves was there as a member of the household staff. We were waiting for Irving to commence. "We are expecting one more party," Irving explained. Suddenly in walked George Radcliff and the lady who sat next to Charles at the funeral. At that time I couldn't see her face because of her hat. I noticed her now. She had an uncanny resemblance to my mother. "Sorry to be late. I had some urgent business to attend to," was George's excuse as he took the unoccupied seat next to Charles. The lady with the hat sat next to me.

It was eerie. Was she a ghost? Do the dead arise from a watery grave? I wasn't sure what was happening here. My mother was dead. Her body was cremated, I thought to myself. Suddenly I began to feel faint and as I got up to excuse myself to use the bathroom, I fell to the floor.

I awoke to hushed, muffled voices. I wasn't in the lawyer's office anymore. I was back at home. The voices I heard were my father's and our family Doctor, Dr. Frances Dorian who made house calls. She had known me since I was a small child. I was in my bed, still in my work clothes. The hearing! "What happened dad? How did I end up here? I was at a Will reading," I tried to explain.

"Rusty, you fainted," my dad began. "Stan brought you home."

"Stan?" I questioned. "Is he still here?"

"Now Rusty, just rest," Dr. Dorian requested. "Daniel, make sure she stays put," she ordered, as she looked at me. She left with that familiar black bag I remember so fondly.

"Wait a minute dad. I was at an important reading and I saw mom," I said in a confused tone. "She was there, in a hat." I admit that sounded ridiculous. My mom is dead, I know she is dead! "The reading of the Will was postponed. You scared everyone Rusty, including an old man like me." Daniel said, adding, "Lt. Levitt said he will contact you when the reading is back on."

I lay back on my soft pillow. "I will get you some ginger ale, Rusty," Daniel said. While my dad was gone I took a warm bubble bath and changed into my favorite pajama's all the while thinking of that woman I saw wearing a big hat. I finally allowed myself to fall asleep in my comfy bed and dreamt of my mom. She had mysteriously drowned. I knew my mom was a good swimmer. It just didn't make sense to me how she died. I never saw her body. My dad told me she was cremated. If she was still alive, then why didn't she contact us? Or was this her way of contacting me?

Two days had passed since my dramatic collapse on the floor. I felt better now and called Lauren. "I heard what happened," Lauren said, adding, "It's on the front page of the newspaper." I suddenly realized the article must have been from Stan Gertz. He was quick to print the fall of Rusty Parker. "I am ok, maybe a little over tired," I tried to explain. Lauren assured, "We are covering things on this end, Rusty" and hung up.

With a well check from Dr. Dorian, I was able to return to work. I inquired about the reading of the Will. Lt. Levitt explained I wasn't invited and he was sending Gavin Cain instead. "Parker, you are too emotional right now. Gavin and I are going tomorrow," Lt Levitt said and that was the end of that discussion.

The next day I got up early and looked in on my dad. He was asleep. I was thinking of my mom. What really happened to her? I fell asleep again on the couch with her photo in my hand. The ringing telephone woke me up. It was Stan. "Rusty, I understand you weren't allowed to come to the reading. Lt. Levitt and Gavin Cain just arrived." I looked at the clock. It was 9:00 AM.

"Are you rubbing it in Stan?" I said, annoyed.

"No. If I leave my cell phone on, you can listen to the reading," Stan explained.

"Stan, that's brilliant. Thanks, I could almost kiss you," I said.

"As long as you don't punch me again, Rusty, like you did in Kindergarten." We both laughed at the recollection.

Stan placed his phone on the table. Nobody questioned why it was there. Stan was with the media and could have used that as an excuse if he needed an explanation. Lt. Levitt and Gavin sat down to chat with Stan. Everyone else walked in and found their seats, including Charles, River and Skyler. Irving Kaplan took his seat and the reading began.

"I have the last Will and Testament of a Ms. Sylvia Elaine Crawford," Irving began. "She has the majority of her money in stocks and bonds that she wished to be divided between Sklyer and River, along with the house. She also left money to the household staff. The yacht, Blue Angel, is bequeathed to Mr. George Radcliff." Irving looked towards George and stated, "The yacht is now yours after all these years." There was a gasp from Charles. Irving read on, "Finally, the lighthouse will be given to Mr. Daniel Parker." Rusty exclaimed to herself, "What, to my dad?" The gasping sounds were now from me. There was no mention of Charles. I heard Irving excuse himself and leave.

Stan came back on the phone, "Rusty, did you hear any of that?" he asked. "Yes," I said. I thanked him and hung up.

As soon as Daniel awoke, Rusty shared the news. He had been given the lighthouse. I checked in with Lt. Levitt who requested my prompt presence the next morning. "Parker, your father was bequeathed the Crawford lighthouse," he said. I tried to look surprised. Lt. Levitt asked,

"Did Daniel know Sylvia Crawford?"

"Yes, my dad designed the lighthouse. That's all I know Lt.," I answered. It stumped me. Why would Sylvia want my dad to have it?

I asked Lt. Levitt if the lady with the big hat was at the reading. He told me no, that I was just imagining things. "Parker, are you sure you want to be back at work?" he asked. I nodded yes and went to my cubicle. Gavin as well as Lauren came over to check on me. I assured them that I was fine. I told them I had listened to the reading of the Will. They asked how? I explained what Stan Gertz had done for me.

"So it looks like Charles Morgan could have had a grudge. He seemed more like Sylvia's house servant than her husband. Like he was beneath her," Lauren said.

Gavin chipped in, "He was below her; he was socially inept, until they married. The tables though have turned because Charles is now above her. He rose to the top of the family legacy." Gavin added, "He came from no money, no social background and married into a fortune."

Lt. Levitt then said, "But Sylvia left him nothing. He started out as a poor man, and ended up as a poor soul."

"What about George Radcliff? What was his connection with the yacht, Blue Angel?" Rusty asked. Lt. Levitt called him to come in for questioning. I pulled out all my research on George Radcliff and found out that he and Sylvia had gone to the same college. I also noticed a picture of them standing together on the deck of the "Blue Angel," the same yacht that George was bequeathed. In the photo, they looked rather chummy. They were holding hands.

George arrived in a whimsical mood. "Good Day, Ms. Parker, your Lt. called me in."

"I know I made the request. Please have a seat." Lt. Levitt came in and sat down next to me. "Mr. Radcliff, why didn't you tell us you knew Sylvia in college?" I asked.

"Ms. Parker, you never asked," was his reply. I remembered the Tahitian necklace and asked George about it. "I don't know what you are talking about," he answered. I showed him the photo of her wearing it.

"Charles reported that it was stolen the night Sylvia's body was found," Lt. Levitt said.

"How well did you know Sylvia in college?" I asked.

"We were engaged," George answered.

"Then how did she end up marrying Charles Morgan?" I asked.

"That Ms. Parker still baffles me. One day we were to marry and the next thing I know, she eloped with Charles Morgan. I was devastated and never truly got over her," George said.

"Have you been holding a grudge all these years?" asked Lt. Levitt.

"I was always resentful that she broke my heart," George replied.

"That must have made you mad enough to kill her," was Lt. Levitt's accusation. George didn't reply. He was arrested, handcuffed and put in a squad car by two men in blue for further questioning. The jail was in another section of town. It seemed too easy. There must be more to the story. I looked to Lt. Levitt. "Leave it alone, Parker," he demanded.

Being the sort of person I am, I couldn't let this case rest. It just didn't feel right. My gut had a strange feeling. So I talked it over with Lauren at lunch. My stomach was aching for food while my heart was yearning for the truth. I ordered a Reuben sandwich and chips from Frank's Deli; Lauren just had a Cobb salad. I told myself I would go back on my diet and exercise routine once I was in a better mood.

I asked Lauren, "What would George Radcliff's motive be? I really don't think he killed Sylvia."

Lauren replied, "Rusty, Lt. Levitt feels that he arrested the right person and wants to wrap up this case." I had to prove it on my own. Was the missing piece to this puzzle the mystery woman in that hat? I have seen her several times since. Why did she look so much like my mom? After lunch, Lauren went back to work. "Are you coming, Rusty?" she asked.

"No, I need to talk to my dad. Please let Lt. Levitt know," Rusty answered.

Daniel Parker was working on his own puzzle when Rusty arrived. "Rusty, this crossword puzzle question has me stumped. He had his ballpoint pen in hand, nervously shaking it. "What is another word for mysterious? It begins with an S." Daniel asked. I looked at his puzzle.

"Try supernatural," I said. The word was a perfect fit. I had my own supernatural feeling and expressed it. "Dad, I keep seeing mom."

"That is only natural, Rusty, she is always with us," was Daniel's explanation.

"Not to change the subject but I was wondering dad, who commissioned you to design the Crawford lighthouse? I believe Sylvia used it as her art studio." The name he gave me was even a greater mystery.

By the next day, Rusty had contacted Lt. Levitt to request permission to search the Crawford lighthouse. "You're like a dog with a bone, Parker," he joked. I explained my feelings on why I needed to be part of it and couldn't let this case rest. The lighthouse was still sealed off as a crime scene when we arrived. The body where Sylvia had lain was etched in chalk. I looked up those steps and as I was about to climb, Charles and his delinquent sons tried to stop us. Lt. Levitt began, "We are here to search the lighthouse. We could do this the easy way and have you lead us to the top, or I can take you all in for obstruction of justice."

Charles nodded to Skyler to let us pass and asked, "This was Sylvia's studio. What do you hope to discover?"

Lt. Levitt answered, "Perhaps the truth."

Skyler led us up the steps with Charles in tow. River stayed back. "To be on guard," he explained. The door had a combination lock on it. Charles quickly punched in the code and the door swung open. It all seemed normal. There was an easel, paints, and all the supplies needed for an artist. There was also modeling clay on a table and what I noticed was a paring knife, probably for slicing clay. It looked to be washed recently. The clay figure next to it reminded me of those structures I made in my sandbox days with Stan. I smiled at the memory. I discovered some sketches of Sylvia's work. Not bad I thought, mostly of still life.

Charles reported that Sylvia's instructor was Edwin Villa. According to Charles, they met at the lighthouse often. My smile faded and muffled my scream when I turned over a canvas with a watercolor painting. "Parker, what's the matter?" asked Lt. Levitt. "Rusty, Rusty!" he shouted. I began to feel faint and fell to the floor. Lt. Levitt and Gavin helped me up and brought me over to a sofa. Lauren gazed upon the painting and remarked, "What is so shocking about this picture?" she asked, "It's just a woman in a hat."

After I was settled, Lt. Levitt came to look and said, "This lady looks like Rustys mom. Rusty fainted before, at the hearing. She thought she saw her mother there too."

"Who painted that portrait?" Lauren asked. Gavin looked at the signature. It was Edwin Villa.

"What happened?" I asked as I awoke in my bed the following morning. My dad was next to me and explained, "You fainted again. Lauren brought you home. Rusty, should I be worried?"

"Yes," was my silent reply.

Edwin Villa was called in for questioning. Lt. Levitt contacted Daniel to keep Rusty home. "I don't know if I could do that, Lt. Rusty is awfully hard headed. She is just as stubborn as her mom," Daniel joked. Rusty was already dressed and out the door before her dad had a chance to say a word.

"Rusty, I told your dad to keep you home," Lt. Levitt said as I entered the lab.

"I don't know why I keep seeing my mom. I know she is dead. Maybe she is trying to give me a message," Rusty rationalized.

"I summoned Edwin Villa. Maybe he can find the missing piece of the puzzle," explained Lt. Levitt, adding, "He should be here soon. Now Rusty, are you going to faint again?" he quipped.

"No sir, I will fight the urge," I joked.

Edwin Villa didn't come across to me as an art teacher. He was well dressed. I guessed he was from the Navajo Indian decent. He had that regal nose. I was instructed by Lt. Levitt not to mention my mom and to stay on task. Edwin was the first to speak. He looked directly at me, "It's you." I realize that Navajo Indians see spirits, though he was looking at me as if I were a ghost.

Lt. Levitt came to my aid. "This is Rusty Parker; she is part of our CSI team."

Edwin said, "You look just like Cordelia." Strange, did he know my mom? Edwin then proceeded to show me a picture of my mom, the one with the hat. As I took a closer look, the lady looked more like Sylvia Crawford.

"How do you know my mom?" I asked.

"Have you been seeing her too?" Edwin asked.

"Yes, and she is always wearing a fancy hat." It sounded silly. I explained, "My mom never wore hats."

"However, Sylvia did. She had a new one every time we met for our art class," Edwin said.

I looked at Lt. Levitt and realized I could not keep my word and not talk about my mom. "I will ask Sylvia's maid, Dorcas Sanders, to bring in some of her hats. Maybe they are the same as you have been seeing Parker," Lt. Levitt said.

Edwin was a religious man. "I come from a long line of Navajo Indians. We believe strongly in the spiritual world. We believe that the dead can take on another form, be another person, one that's more comforting and familiar to a loved one. It makes it easier to cope. Maybe your vision of your mother is really Sylvia's ghost, asking for your help to solve this case."

Was it true? Was the lady in the hat really Sylvia's ghost? "Look inside yourself, Evelyn. The truth shall set you free," Edwin said and then he was gone in a blink of an eye. But how did he know my real name? I wondered.

Back at the CSI building, Lauren was finally granted a warrant from Commissioner Bedford to search George Radcliff's yacht. The search of the lighthouse proved that Edwin Villa and Sylvia Crawford might have known Cordelia Parker in some capacity. How were they connected?

Lauren had the results of the fingerprint analysis. The prints lifted from Sylvia's neck weren't a good reading. The DNA under Sylvia's nails was inconclusive. Back to the drawing board, Lauren thought. She handed in all her results to Commissioner Bedford as he handed her the warrant saying, "I don't think Rusty should be involved. Please keep this quest between you, Cain, Levitt and myself," Lauren nodded that she understood.

Rusty was anxious being back at work. Since she had fainted twice now, she knew she had to have a strong disposition. She didn't realize her co-workers were conspiring to protect her, since she kept fainting. Rusty walked into Lt. Levitt's office inquiring about her next assignment. She felt a cold reception, even from him. Lt. Levitt spoke, "Parker, you are one of our best agents. A lot has been happening with this case and I don't want it compromised. Mathews and Cain are going to search George Radcliff's yacht. I need you here while I question Sylvia's maid,

Dorcas Sanders." Lt. Levitt probably assumed I would be safer here at the lab. I didn't want to jeopardize the case so I agreed.

Before Ms. Sanders came in, she telephoned the Lt. to explain that Sylvia wore several different styles of hats and inquired what he was actually looking for. Gavin Cain was a bit of a sketch artist and helped draw the hats that Rusty had seen on the mystery woman as Rusty phoned describing every detail. When Gavin finished, he was able to tell Ms. Sanders what hats she was to bring in. Before that could occur though, Lt. Levitt had to be sure of the etchings. He asked Edwin to draw the same pictures to get another interpretation. Dorcas arrived with the hats in question that day. When Gavin had finished, he was excused to help Lauren.

Gavin met Lauren at the loading dock to check out the yacht, "Blue Angel." With George in jail, it made their job a little easier. The yacht was moored in a private club called, "The Salty Dogs." George and the manager, Troy Windward, had the combination to the lock below. Troy approached Lauren and Gavin asking if he could be of some assistance. "We have a warrant to search this vessel," Gavin explained, asking, "Is this the yacht George Radcliff stays on?"

"What is this all about?" asked Troy.

"Mr. Radcliff is involved in an ongoing police investigation. We need this lock opened so we can have a look around," Gavin stated. Troy immediately opened the lock as he looked to Lauren and said, "Ladies first."

Lauren walked down the steps to the cabin bellow noticing everything. It was custom made with handcrafted furniture and Spanish tile on the counter tops. It definitely had a woman's touch. There was a picture mounted on the wall of Sylvia Crawford and George Radcliff on the yacht's deck. It was the same picture Rusty had seen during her research on Sylvia, Lauren remembered. Lauren also saw a small watercolor painting of a sailboat docked by the Back Bay Beach. Edwin Villa had painted it.

Lauren noticed a chart with three points marked that looked like a triangle. That same shape was on Sylvia's back. While wearing gloves, she rolled the chart and secured it with a rubber band. Everything seemed to be wiped clean; everything seemed to be in order. With camera in hand, Lauren took pictures of her findings, even the wall picture.

Gavin was consumed by the yacht's galley. He

realized that it was bigger than his entire apartment. Everything a cook would desire. Even the cutlery was properly placed. He noted that one of the knives was missing from its block. The slot was small, perhaps to fit a paring knife?

Lauren recalled Rusty had found a small knife in the lighthouse studio. Edwin Villa explained it to be a tool for slicing clay. George's missing knife could have been used for a slicing too, perhaps for slicing up Sylvia Crawford?

Back at the lab the team compared notes. Lt. Levitt wrote down on an easel the facts as he explained them, "Fact number 1.) Sylvia Crawford was found murdered on the top step of the lighthouse. Fact number 2.) She was stabbed three times. Fact number 3.) The lighthouse was built ten years ago and designed by Daniel Parker. Fact number 4.) George Radcliff had known Sylvia Crawford in college; they were engaged and had a yacht together, the Blue Angel. Fact number 5.) Edwin Villa gave Sylvia Crawford private art lessons in the lighthouse." Gavin then jested, "Perhaps there was more to it than just painting?"

Lauren looked at Gavin then at Lt. Levitt stating, "Maybe she was having a fling with Edwin. We know she broke her engagement to George

Radcliff when she married Charles Morgan."

"Still how is Rusty Parker involved? We found out at the Will reading that Daniel Parker was bequeathed the lighthouse that he originally designed. Rusty keeps seeing her mother." Lt. Levitt pondered adding, "Let's go talk to Daniel and Rusty and make it off the record."

Rusty was still in her pajama's by 1:00 PM. With her tea in her hand, she sat down with her dad. "Rusty, are you going to get dressed today?" Daniel asked.

"No, I don't feel like it," was Rusty's sarcastic explanation. She stared at the TV as she added, "Dad, they don't seem to want me at the station anymore." Daniel handed his best girl the clicker and she turned on her favorite Soap, "One Life To Live."

Just at the Soap's crucial cliffhanger moment, the doorbell rang at Rusty's abode. "Just let it ring dad. I need to know what will happen to the lives of Landview." Rusty anxiously tried to explain. Daniel opened the door as Rusty heard the soaps theme song conclude. "Oh, Lt. Levitt, Gavin and Lauren, this is indeed a surprise," Daniel said in a happy tone as he looked to me. I wasn't too cheerful as I donned my pink robe and fuzzy slippers, slumping into my chair.

"Daniel, we are here to ask you questions about the Crawford lighthouse." Lt. Levitt began, "We know you were the original designer. What we are curious about is how you originally knew Sylvia Crawford."

"She and Cordelia were cousins. I met Sylvia when I met my wife," Daniel responded.

"May I be excused?" asked Rusty.

"Parker, we need you back to work pronto. But first get dressed," ordered Lt. Levitt. My robe and my body were beginning to feel itchy anyway.

With Rusty looking more rested and alive, it was a good time to discuss the weary and the dead. "I understand Parker that this has been a difficult case for you. I believe you are the key we need to open this Pandora's Box." Lt. Levitt began adding, "Let's start at the beginning. Daniel, please explain your relationship to Sylvia Crawford. Did she commission you to design the lighthouse?"

"Yes," was Daniel's response as he looked at me. "There is more to it than that, Rusty. Sylvia

Crawford was blackmailing your mom. You see, Sylvia knew your mom quite well. I couldn't tell you all the facts leading to your mom's death because Sylvia was involved." I looked at my dad and for the very first time; he had become a stranger to me.

"What?" Rusty exclaimed.

"Maybe we should take your statement at headquarters to make it more official," Lt. Levitt requested. I remained silent in my dad's car as we drove to the station staring straight ahead, lost in my memories. My mom drowned five years ago. I just found out she was related to Sylvia Crawford, they shared the same genetic DNA. "Rusty, I am sorry I kept the truth from you," Daniel began. Tears streamed down my face. I still didn't understand. As soon as we reached the CSI building, I ran into the ladies room. Staring at my reflection in the mirror, I saw the lady in the hat. I quickly turned around to look and saw no one there. I looked at the mirror again; the face I saw was my own. The lady in the hat was me.

"How were Sylvia and my mom cousins?" Rusty asked her dad as she entered Lt. Levitt's office. Daniel explained, "Your mom's mom and Sylvia Crawford's mom were sisters."

Rusty noted, "During my research on this case, I read that Sylvia's mom was an opera singer. Sylvia lived as a girl on that estate where she died."

I didn't know much of my mom's mother. My dad never shared that information with me. Maybe I had to find my own answers. I had to dive deep into the past to discover why my mom drowned. I planned on using the computer at the library the next day to look for any information on a Cordelia Ann Roberts. My dad and I drove back home the way we came, in silence.

The days were longer now since it was summer. Living by the coastline, the weather was never too hot. Tourists arrived by boatloads, either by private or passenger vessels to visit the Isle of Cortez. The merchants, who lived in my town of Annabillow, saw a lot of action. We had nice quality restaurants and shops. My dad and I frequented Joe's Fish Café where we were known as local celebrities. Annabillow was known for their fresh fish. Out at the harbor, one could see boats returning from an early catch, mostly commercial and local fishermen. The skies were filled with seagulls looking for a bite to eat. Though I enjoy eating fish, I am glad I don't have to clean or cook them. If you listen carefully, one can hear the sounds of foghorns from passing ships on foggy nights. Their song was sweet music to my ears.

On the high terrain of The Isle of Cortez, wild buffalo wandered as well deer. The visitors, who came by bus, could ride and see the native wild animals. Benny had the job of tour director for about fifteen years and loved his job. Merchants were counting on the tourists returning year after year for that was their means of survival.

The tourists were coming to Annabillow now for another reason. Charles Morgan and his sons were the newest celebrities in town. They couldn't go anywhere without the press hounding them. Their latest yarn was the news that Daniel Parker had known Sylvia Crawford. The media assumed they were having an affair. Stan Gertz approached Charles one morning as he was leaving his home with Skyler. "Excuse me sir, do you deny the rumors about your late wife and Daniel Parker?" Stan added, "Why would Sylvia give Daniel the lighthouse?" Charles looked at Stan as a flash went off from the Annabillow Anecdotes photographer, Brooke Burke. Charles noticed the pretty young thing.

Skyler was quick to shield the lens as Charles

exclaimed, "I will not answer any questions. Now please stop hounding me, my sons and my household staff." Charles gave a cordial nod to Brooke as he left with Skyler.

Skyler and River were in their last year of college. Sklyer lived at home, River choose to stay at the dorm. It was too hard for him to be at home, too many memories. River checked in on Sundays, collect of course, to see if there had been any breaks in his mother's murder. Charles reported to him that George Radcliff had been arrested.

Charles took his scotch to his den and sat down in his favorite chair. He picked up a picture on the end table and looked at it lovingly. It was not of his late wife, but of her cousin, Cordelia Roberts. Charles had a long secret crush on Cordelia but she broke his heart by marrying Daniel Parker. He met Cordelia, Sylvia's cousin at a spring dance many moons ago. Charles only had eyes for Cordelia but married Sylvia because of her family legacy, her family's money and the Crawford name.

Cordelia and her cousin Sylvia spent their summers as children and young adults at the Back Bay Beach. Sylvia was very popular with the boys, always flirting and teasing them, as Cordelia was a little reserved. "Come on Cordelia," Sylvia prompted one afternoon in 1963. "The water is fantastic," Sylvia exaggerated. Cordelia was a champion swimmer at the time whereas Sylvia was not. Sylvia got in too deep that day, to the point of almost drowning. It was Cordelia who pulled her out and administered CPR. Sylvia gasped for air and didn't even bother thanking her cousin. "Get off of me," she growled between breaths. There to witness this amazing feat were not only the lifeguards and bystanders, but also Daniel Parker.

Cordelia met the man of her dreams that day at Back Bay Beach. Sylvia met the hand and a lecture from her parents. After being publicly humiliated for the last time by his daughter, Braden Crawford arranged the marriage between Sylvia and Charles Morgan. Braden also gave Charles a job in his firm as an apprentice. He felt Sylvia needed to be humbled and controlled. He knew that Charles was the perfect man for that task. Charles' mother Dorothy even designed Sylvia's wedding dress. Cordelia Roberts was a bridesmaid and her dress was made to synchronize with Sylvia's.

The neighborhood library is where Lauren found Rusty doing her research. Rusty had been there several times since she last spoke with Lauren.

"Your dad told me I'd find you here," Lauren said adding, "I miss you at work."

"I miss you too Lauren and the team. I have been consumed with this case," Rusty said.

"Maybe we should spin it out," Lauren jokingly suggested. Perhaps exercise would help me blow off some steam, I thought to myself.

"Ok, when is the next class?" Rusty eagerly asked.

"In forty-five minutes," Lauren answered as she rushed Rusty out the door.

After the class Lauren and I went to our favorite deli. This time I ordered the Cobb Salad. I felt back in the game, ready to move on. I thanked Lauren and then drove home. My new plan was to find out everything about my grandmother. She was a sister of Sylvia Crawford's mother, Andrea. With the materials I checked out from the library, I went to work. Andrea was an acclaimed opera singer. Wagner and Pucchini were her specialties. She met Braden backstage after taking her last bow as the curtain fell during a performance. He presented her with roses and a proposal. Cordelia's mom, Josephine, a stage actress, was a Crawford too but changed her last name to Roberts when she married Lt. Dean Roberts, an Admiral in the Navy. Josephine married Dean in 1923 in the rose garden of the Crawford estate. They looked happy in the photo I had discovered. Cordelia was born October 28th, 1932. I read she was a blue baby. She had to overcome a lot of childhood illnesses. Sylvia was born before Cordelia in that same year on June 7th. They were about four months apart. Both girls were the only children in their families.

Josephine Crawford Roberts was my grand-mother, thought Rusty as she looked at the photo. Cordelia was her daughter and my mother. I never met my grandmother. She died the year I was born, 1965. She must have been striking. In her early photos she resembled Vivien Leigh with her dark raven hair and piercing blue eyes. I too had the same eye color. I read she drowned by walking out to the white caps of the sea after the doctors discovered she had leukemia. A fisherman discovered her body days later washed upon the shore. Josephine had never learned to swim. It was improper for women in those days to learn. Josephine's husband, Dean, died the year before, in 1964 of natural causes. Josephine was buried next to Dean in the family crypt. How interesting? Rusty pondered, because my mother mysteriously drowned too.

Sylvia Crawford's parents went on to live a long healthy life. Braden was 90 when he passed away displaying early stages of Parkinson's and Andrea was 75 and died in her sleep, the cause unknown.

It was too much of a coincidence that both my mom and grandmother took their own lives, I thought. My grandmother had leukemia. Did my mom also have leukemia? I pondered. I never knew the truth. It was time for another talk with my dad. Daniel was asleep in his chair when Rusty arrived home; her past was brewing in her thoughts. "It can keep till morning," Rusty murmured as she kissed her dad goodnight.

Deep in sleep, Rusty dreamt of her mom again. Over at the Crawford house, Skyler and River were wide-awake. The staff still served them and Charles as if nothing had changed. The staff was at Skyler and Rivers beck and call whenever they needed something, no matter how late. The media had stopped hounding them because an arrest had been made. Though George was in jail, Skyler and River often wondered if the right man was behind bars. To appease their curiosity, they decided to visit George the following day.

George still managed to look dapper in his orange jump suit. He seldom received visitors and relished his solitude. George was happily surprised one afternoon when the guard told him he had two visitors waiting for him. He thought maybe it was Ms. Parker? But who was the other? As he sat down behind the glass partition, his warm cordial smile turned cold when he saw who was waiting. It was Skyler and River Crawford.

"Did you kill our mother?" Skyler asked hastily. "We don't believe you did," River added.

George interjected, "I believe the truth killed your dear mama."

"How well did you know our mother?" River asked.

"Intimately," was George's answer adding, "But don't be so quick to accuse your dad of murder. Sylvia had been hiding a secret for a long time. She confided in me because it was destroying her. I feel you should have a chat with Rusty Parker because it involves her mother. Now if you will both excuse me, it's time for my mid-morning art class. Today's lesson is about shades of gray. You see boys; everything is not as black and white as it appears to be." George motioned to the guard to take him back to his cell.

Edwin Villa volunteered his services once a week

at the prison. He was happy to see George, as George was happy to see him. Their common link was that they both knew Sylvia Crawford and Cordelia Parker. Edwin not only gave Sylvia art lessons in the lighthouse but Cordelia was sometimes his model, his muse and often posed in different styles of hats. Cordelia kept this a secret from both Daniel and Rusty. Only Sylvia was in on the secret. Cordelia knew Sylvia was fooling around on Charles and used that as leverage to keep her from telling Daniel and Rusty the truth. The secret about Cordelia wasn't about her modeling for Edwin, but the fact she was dying; she had diabetes. The legs that had supported her through her swimming career were slowing her down, rapidly. Sylvia hid the truth about her cousin Cordelia to save her marriage. Sylvia's father had written in his Will that if Sylvia wanted her inheritance, she had to stay married to Charles Morgan.

Charles was reading in his study when Sklyer and River came home later that evening. Anges announced their arrival, which startled Charles. "Thank you Anges," Charles acknowledged.

"Very good sir, will there be anything else you desire before I retire? Perhaps some brandy?"

"No thank you Anges. Good night," Charles

replied. Agnes shut the door to the study behind him.

"Skyler, where have you been?" Charles asked in an accusing tone. Skyler ignored him and went to his room. River stayed behind and reported, "Dad we went to go talk to George Radcliff."

Charles looked betrayed. "For what purpose?" he asked.

"I wanted to know if he really did kill mom or if he knew who did. George suggested we talk to Rusty Parker," River said.

"The gal with the CSI team?" asked Charles.

"I don't know why but maybe we should have a talk with her," River replied.

The dawn always comes up like thunder was an expression my mom often used. Early signs of light fell to the tips of the mountains cascading into the seas of Annabillow. The radiant colors of the sunrise led into a tangerine sky. They suddenly changed to red as the Crawford lighthouse was soon ablaze. The smell of the smoke was as suffocating as the hands of death, its flames grabbing for our throats. The alarms in the bedrooms at the Crawford house sounded because the fumes lingered in the air. The point of origin wasn't clear to Charles; he just knew to get his family out. It was Anges who called 911 after discovering the fire when he took Ronrico out for his morning walk.

The Staff as well as Charles, Skyler and River looked in awe to the enormous beast before them. Blasting sirens came to a screeching halt as firemen went to work trying to control the monster that surrounded the lighthouse. Within hours the fire was finally put out. The concrete steps were the only structure still standing. The lighthouse was destroyed. Onlookers passed by when the smoke cleared. The only man who stayed behind was Stan Gertz. He was the first to call Rusty.

"It's on the news Stan, thanks," Rusty said.

"Are you coming over here?" he asked. "Your team is already here."

They didn't even bother to tell me, Rusty thought. "I will be right there Stan." Rusty told her dad about Stan's call. He was watching the story unfold on the local news. The anchor mentioned arson was the possible source of the outbreak. Rusty was soon out the door with her camera in hand.

Lt. Levitt had the area roped off. It seemed like Déjà Vous, like the time when Sylvia Crawford's body was found. Now it was arson that brought us all back to this particular site. "Lt. Levitt, why didn't you call me?" asked Rusty.

"Parker, I didn't want you involved. You are too close to this case. Cain and Matthews are here. We are covered," explained Lt. Levitt.

"I just don't like being left out of the investigation," Rusty said. I did sound childish. Maybe they were right. My dad designed the Crawford lighthouse. His pride and joy were gone.

"Parker, I promise that I will call you if we find something that needs your attention," Lt. Levitt assured her.

"Do you remember when you were a child and you didn't get your way, Rusty? You looked just like how you are looking now, down to the pouty lip and growl upon your face." I turned to see Stan's eyes upon mine. "Come on, Rusty. Let me buy you a bite to eat. It will make up for all the endless teasing you had to endure from me in school," joked Stan.

After consulting with Daniel, Stan found out

that Rusty's favorite breakfast restaurant was Blueberry Hill. Between bites she had a chance to really see Stan. He was a nerdy kid. He liked bugs and mud as well as Rusty did. He was always getting in trouble for kissing the pretty girls. It was Rusty though, that hit him back every time he tried. Stan was all grown up now. The nerdy kid turned out all right, rather good looking. "What are you staring at Rusty?" asked Stan.

"Just remembering our sandbox days," Rusty answered with a sly smile on her face. Stan's eyes were hidden behind dark glasses. He had that Clark Kent look to him. Maybe someday he would show Rusty his alter ego because he never stopped loving her, ever since she hit him so long ago. A boy's childhood crush had escalated to real feelings for her. Their thoughts lingered throughout breakfast.

Afterwards Rusty returned home hoping for a call from two men, Stan Gertz and Lt. Jack Levitt. Her phone instantly rang. It was Lt. Levitt. "Parker, the fire destroyed everything. The turpentine we found was used as an accelerant. All the paintings were destroyed beyond recognition." I wondered about the painting of the lady in the hat and asked Lt. Levitt. He answered, "I am not sure how many paintings were inside the lighthouse but I will have Edwin

Villia have a look to see if any are missing. Parker, I need you back here permanently. I am sorry for being so stubborn," he admitted. Lt. Levitt and I were a lot alike in that way.

"Ok, where do you need me, sir?" asked Rusty.

"Here with the team at the arson site," Lt. Levitt added, "Parker, bring your camera. You take better pictures than any of us." With an apology and a compliment, things were looking brighter. Daniel was sitting in his chair reading the paper as Rusty kissed his cheek, took a sip of his coffee and ran out the door.

The steps that led to the lighthouse were the only structures still intact, Rusty noticed as she snapped a picture. Lt. Levitt was talking to Edwin Villa who had been summoned by him to help look through the paintings or what was left of them. "What a dreadful mess, everything is gone. My beautiful paintings," Edwin sadly said. "I had codes on all my paintings. They would match what I have here." Edwin took out a sheet of paper from his left pocket. Edwin explained, "Let me see if I can trace them." He sounded hopeful. Edwin had twelve paintings stored in the lighthouse; the others were at his apartment. Edwin went through what he could manage, most of the paintings were nothing but crisp remains, he tried to hold back his tears.

Can I help, Mr. Villa?" asked Rusty.

"Yes, thanks. That would be great." Within hours Edwin found codes of just eleven paintings as he reported his findings. "Lt. Levitt, It's very hard to tell but as you see Ms. Parker and I were able to salvage what we could. Most of the paper is charcoal now but the frames are ok. You see, they are made from brass, which doesn't burn as easily as paper. The frames have codes on them and match the paintings, or what were the paintings. Only eleven frames are accounted for. One is missing. I can tell you what the painting was because of the code of that missing frame," Edwin explained.

"Which painting was it?" asked Lt. Levitt.

Edwin looked towards Rusty, "It was my favorite. It was of your mother, Ms. Parker. She was modeling an exquisite hat."

"What, my mother wasn't a model," exclaimed Rusty!

Edwin explained, "Sylvia Crawford was my art student for years. I gave her art lessons here at the lighthouse." Edwin looked around and shook his head because it was gone. "Your mother as a favor to Sylvia modeled for us. Cordelia looked a lot like you, Ms. Parker. You have the same sadness in your eyes. Cordelia kept her modeling a secret, only Sylvia knew besides me of course. She wanted it that way so I kept it quiet. She didn't model for long. She stopped when she found out she was pregnant with you, Ms. Parker," Edwin explained.

I felt Ms. Parker sounded too formal. "Please call me Rusty, Mr. Villa."

"And please call me Edwin," he added.

"Edwin, I knew my mom was a swimmer. She gave up that career to have me. That is what she told me," Rusty said in a confused tone.

Edwin explained, "She was doing both at the time. Her swimming schedule kept her busy during her day but she came to me at night because that is when Sylvia could get away. Sylvia was very persuasive towards her cousin and demanded that Cordelia oblige. She must have had something on her to make her pose because I could tell Cordelia didn't really want to. Though Cordelia never confided in me about Sylvia's blackmail, she did often talk about wanting a child. Finally, she got her wish as G-d blessed her with you,

Evelyn, and her whole world changed."

"How do you know my real name?" Rusty asked.

"I helped your mother choose it," Edwin answered.

Lt. Levitt came to my aid because I was speechless. Lt. Levitt explained, "The same person who took that missing painting is probably the same person who started this fire."

Skyler and River Morgan were waiting at the station when Lt. Levitt and Rusty returned. It was late, almost closing time. "Ms. Parker, may we have a word?" asked Skyler.

"I am sorry; it is not a good time. Please come back in the morning and I will be glad to talk with you," answered Rusty.

"It won't take long," River pleaded with a look of desperation in his eyes.

Rusty looked to Lt. Levitt who said, "All right, but make it quick. I will give you fifteen minutes" and he left.

"Please have a seat. Now what is so urgent?" asked Rusty.

"We went to visit George Radcliff. He said that we needed to talk to you about our mother's murder. George told us there was a secret that only you knew," Skyler said.

"My mother and your mother, Sylvia were cousins. That would make us second cousins," Rusty explained.

Both Skyler and River looked confused. "Is that the big secret?" River asked.

"Edwin Villa was your mother's art teacher and my mother was one of his models. Sylvia kept a secret about my mom from my dad and me. It involved both George Radcliff and Edwin Villa. Both men knew our mothers quite well. It was assumed that Sylvia was having an affair with both George and Edwin. My mother's secret was that she had diabetes and only wanted her cousin to know. I just recently found that out from Mr. Villa and the fact my mother modeled for him. George Radcliff must have found out somehow about my mom's illness. I guess Sylvia must have told him in confidenance. He kept that secret about my mom because he never talked to me about it."

"I still don't know how you are involved, Rusty?

River said, adding, "Did your mother know George Radcliff?"

"I'm not sure. Perhaps he knew of my mom's illness without Sylvia having to tell him. My mom was kind to everyone and made friends easily and maybe she confided in him, but why? I guess I need to talk to George again." Rusty assured. At that moment, Lt. Levitt came back in announcing that the time was up. Skyler and River thanked Rusty and left.

"I am going to have to let George Radcliff go, Rusty. He just posted bail," Lt. Levitt said.

"Who posted it?" Rusty asked.

"Guess?" was his reply.

The lighthouse is where this mystery began. Sylvia Crawford was found brutally murdered, stabbed three times. A necklace she wore was ripped off her neck leaving puncture marks. That necklace had been reported stolen. People of interest in this case are Charles Morgan, George Radcliff, and Edwin Villa. They all knew Sylvia Crawford and had the motive and opportunity to kill her. Was Sylvia Crawford my Great Aunt? She was my mother's cousin. I am confused. My birth name, Evelyn, means shinning light, like a beacon to help fisherman and sailors find their way. Like the lighthouse my dad designed. Only this lighthouse was used as a studio, I guess for Sylvia to find her way, for her to have some privacy away from her reality. She met up with both Edwin and George there. She escaped from her ordinary life to find a new purpose, to feel alive again and loved. Only she ended up dead by someone who defiantly wanted her gone.

Charles Morgan stated that he never went near the lighthouse after it was built. The lighthouse was now destroyed. Charles had Sylvia cremated without telling his sons first. Was he trying to conceal something? Maybe another chat with Lauren Mathews would be helpful. She did examine the body before Charles took it. Lauren kept photographs and notes of the body. Rusty was hopeful as she left Lt. Levitt's office later that evening.

The following day, Rusty was at Lauren's cubicle. "Lauren, I need to see your report on Sylvia Crawford when she was first brought in. You shared with me about the markings on her neck as well as the three points on her upper back. Charles Morgan had her cremated soon after he was given back the body from the coroner." I remarked, asking, "I wonder why Charles was in such a hurry? He didn't even give his sons an opportunity to say their good-byes."

Within a few hours, Lauren had her notes gathered and presented them to Rusty at her workspace. She asked, "What are you looking for?"

"Another piece to the puzzle," answered Rusty.

Back at the Crawford house, Charles Morgan had some unresolved issues. He had always suspected that Sylvia had a secret that involved her cousin Cordelia. He ventured in Sylvia's room pondering his thoughts. The room remained untouched. Her maid Dorcas still pressed the sheets on her bed and kept things in order down to the fresh gardenias on her nightstand personally picked by Anges. Her terrace window overlooked the area where the lighthouse had once stood. The curtains were opened and closed by Dorcas every day. Sylvia's clothes still hung in her closet as well as her hats. Charles wanted it that way, to keep Sylvia's spirit alive for her sons. As he entered Sylvia's room one morning, he opened the wall safe in her closet. He threw papers all over the floor out of sheer desperation. After reading over the papers, he found what he was looking for, a document stating that Cordelia Ann Roberts Parker had given Sylvia Elaine Crawford legal permission to end her suffering by any means she found accessible. Charles knew that Cordelia had drowned but also knew she was a champion swimmer. In the document it stated how to end her life if her diabetes was in the advanced stage and there was no hope. Sylvia had a heart after all and spared her cousin from pain, Charles thought. He then felt a bit remorseful for having Sylvia's body cremated so quickly. For he always thought of her as a selfish bitch, not carrying about anyone but herself. Charles cleaned up the mess and placed everything back in the safe and locked it. He then went to his chair in his study and looked at the picture of Cordelia. It was she whom he truly loved.

Rusty looked through Lauren's documents and didn't find anything that would lead them to Sylvia's murderer though she did find a rolled up chart. "Lauren must have forgotten about this." Rusty thought as she placed it next to her. Rusty also jotted down her thoughts in her notebook. The first subject she was thinking about was George Radcliff. That man was an enigma. He lived on the yacht, "Blue Angel" which had later been bequeathed to him by Sylvia Crawford. He knew her intimately. George intended marrying her but she stunned him by marrying Charles Morgan.

Rusty unrolled the chart, noticing the markings. She gathered Lauren, Gavin and Lt. Levitt in her cubicle. "Lauren, what do you make of these markings? You are a sailor, do they make any sense?" asked Rusty.

Lauren looked more closely at the chart. "The three point's match the pattern on Sylvia's back," she explained, adding, "I should have seen it before. At first I said that the marking on Sylvia's back looked like a ships sail and that is why I wanted to search George Radcliff's yacht. These three points on the chart could be something else. They are marked in different locations on a rural road in an Indian community." Lauren explained. Lt. Levitt left to seek a search warrant from the commissioner. Rusty knew where they were going next and wrote down the subject in her notebook.

Edwin Villa lived on an ancient Indian ground in "Red Tree." He was a spiritual man and often felt the presence of the departed. He had a small apartment on Sequoia road where he taught art to the kids. Everyone liked Edwin. Inside his modest one-bedroom apartment, was an art worktable in the kitchen. He would rather paint than cook he often joked. His students sometimes paid him with food and other offerings to help him make ends meet. Edwin relished his private life and enjoyed being isolated from the outside world, though today would be different because there was a knock on his front door. Edwin was surprised to see Lt. Levitt and his team. "Lt., Welcome. Please, why don't you all come in and make yourselves at home." Edwin tried to hide his surprise. Following Lt. Levitt was Rusty, Lauren, and Gavin who began looking around. Edwin asked, "Now what can I do for you?"

Lt. Levitt took out his pad stating, "You can start by explaining why you paid George Radcliff's bail," adding, "I didn't realize you knew each other."

Secrets, this town is full of them! Sylvia Crawford had them. Cordelia Roberts, Charles Morgan and even Daniel Parker had them too. It was Daniel who first introduced Edwin to George. Daniel met George when he was a struggling architecture student in college. Edwin at that time was an art student. George came from a lot of money and power and was a successful entrepreneur, having graduated a year before. He was also engaged to Sylvia Crawford so he had a lot of influences. George saw a lot of potential in both men and helped finance Daniel and Edwin's projects. George liked Daniel's designs and put him to work as soon as he graduated. George commissioned Edwin to paint a picture of a sailboat that was tied to the docks by the Back Bay Beach. George framed the picture and hung it in the yacht, "Blue Angel."

"I knew George when I was a student at ASU, Annabillow State University. He helped me financially get started in my art endeavors after I graduated." Edwin explained. "I paid his bail because George had done so much to help me. I wanted to return the favor." Edwin quickly glanced outside and noticed Gavin nosing around. Edwin said, "Lt, will you please excuse me. I need to see if your team needs anything." He scurried off. Outside Edwin's apartment was a large field, mostly planted vegetables. There was a menacing looking scarecrow in the center of the field. Gavin noticed it and approached it. Lauren and Rusty came outside to look around. It was a nice, open space. There was even a flower garden that had marigolds, roses, and gardenias. Rusty even spotted her favorite ladybugs. She recalled a folklore her dad had once told her when she was young. He explained that ladybugs brought good luck. They eat insects off the crops increasing the harvest. Edwin's luck was running out.

"The scarecrow is supposed to scare off birds and other animals who might want to dig where they are not supposed to," Edwin explained to Gavin.

"Does it work?" asked Gavin.

"I will let you know shortly," was Edwin's quick reply.

Lt. Levitt approached and said, "Thank you Edwin for your time. Your home seems very tranquil." Lt. Levitt and his team left. Edwin breathed a sigh of relief as he closed his front door.

Summer nights turned to autumn days. The sun sets earlier and the air had a crisp feel to it. Leaves changed their colors to reds and golds. It was harvest season in Annabillow. Local farmers sold the crops they had grown to the markets on the Isle of Cortez. Trucks transported them all over the island, stopping first in our town. The drivers always remarked that we were the nicest community. Besides the town of Annabillow, there was a smaller town named "Aviary Row." The nature conservatory resides there. "The Winged Wonders" has hundreds of living butterflies, ladybugs and exotic colorful birds. Tourists from Annabillow motor over for an excursion.

In the village of "Red Tree" there were birds

of prey. Their feathers were woven into dream catchers, a web-like hoop that was used to keep out all the bad dreams, the nightmares of the person who possessed it. Edwin Villa was faithful to his founding fathers and practiced his rituals on a daily basis.

The townsfolk gathered pumpkins for their Halloween rituals. Homes in Annabillow were decorated as children marched around in their favorite costumes. The sacred grounds had restrictions against trespassers, especially on Halloween. It was a known fact that spirits roamed the land on that night.

Rusty liked Halloween as a child. It was different now with her mom gone because she felt her mom's presence; her spirit was always with her. Halloween was commonly known as Dia, de los muertos, the day of the dead. Besides Cordelia's spirit wandering around, Sylvia's was as well. The CSI team celebrated the day too. Lt. Levitt requested that they dress up, to get in the spirit of the carnival. Rusty was Dorothy, Lauren was the cowardly lion, Lt. Levitt was the tin man and Gavin was the scarecrow from "The Wizard of Oz."

Edwin Villa had dressed his scarecrow in his field as a pirate with a treasure chest lying at its feet. Edwin thought he had the key that locked away his secrets. Edwin had very few trick or treaters. His road wasn't well lit; only the moon supplied light that led to his home. The light above his front door was out by 9:00 PM.

By then, Rusty and her team were home. Their costumes were off and they were settling in for a good night's sleep. Scary things happened on this night. Rusty may have been asleep but others were not in the town of Annabillow. Charles Morgan was awake, George Radcliff, as well as Edwin Villa. Their thoughts were of the ladies who died, Cordelia and Sylvia. Those ladies constantly haunted their dreams, becoming their worst nightmares.

November 5th marked Rusty's 43rd birthday. Her father made her Eggs Benedict, which was her favorite. "Happy Birthday Rusty, your mom would be so proud of the beautiful young woman you have become," Daniel said, handing her his gift. Rusty read the card and laughed. She continued smiling when she discovered the gift inside. It was a pair of gold crossed Tiffany earrings her mom always wore.

"Thank you, dad, they are perfect." After breakfast, Daniel and Rusty sat down to catch up on things. Rusty's thoughts drifted to her case.

"Dad, the lighthouse you were given was burned. I still don't understand why Sylvia wanted you to have it; perhaps she knew it was your favorite design."

"Rusty, your mom modeled for Sylvia and Edwin Villa there," Daniel began. I didn't know he was aware of mom's other life. I didn't let on that I already knew. "I guess Sylvia wanted me to have the lighthouse so I could feel closer to Cordelia."

"How did you know mom was a model?" asked Rusty.

Daniel pulled out some of the prints of Cordelia. "Sylvia gave them to me. She thought I would like a part of her cousin that only she knew, though I had known for a while, even before Sylvia told me. Charles Morgan had followed Sylvia to the light house one night and there he found your mom modeling hats. He was quick to tell me about it. I thought it was a nice experience for her to have. I wish she had been honest about it, I wouldn't have minded. Your mom was a beautiful woman, Rusty." Daniel sounded far away, lost in his thoughts of happier days.

I felt close to my mom today. She always had surprises for my birthday. Charles Morgan had a surprise visit from Lt. Levitt. He wasn't happy with Charles and demanded the truth. "Mr. Morgan, your sons have come to me voluntarily and accused you of wanting your wife dead. They think you are hiding something from them about why you had your late wife cremated so quickly," Lt. Levitt said.

"I didn't want my sons to suffer any more than they had already endured. It's hard enough on them that their mother is dead." Charles tried to desperately explain. Charles kept the truth to himself that he secretly loved Cordelia and simply wanted to permanently erase Sylvia from his memory.

"Did you kill your wife Mr. Morgan?" Lt. Levitt asked. Charles had hated Sylvia for a long time. He only married her because he had made a deal with the devil, her father Braden Crawford. Braden knew that Charles would keep his daughter humbled.

"No, I did not kill my wife," was Charles' answer.

"What about your sons Skyler and River?" Lt. Levitt asked.

Was Lt. Levitt grasping at straws? "Why would

they want to kill their mother?" Charles asked out of frustration, adding, "They were her most precious possessions!"

"Are your sons here?" asked Lt. Levitt.

"Are they suspects?" asked Charles. Lt. Levitt knew that they weren't but he wanted to see Charles' reaction. Charles was very protective of his boys; as a father, not as a killer.

"No, they are not suspects. We have questioned George Radcliff and Edwin Villa too. We are just covering every possible angle." Lt. Levitt thanked Charles and left.

A painter props his subjects in several different styles and positions. A medium a painter might use could be acrylic paint, ceramic tiles or even modeling clay. Tools commonly used are a small brush or a small sculpting knife. Edwin Villa started as a young boy decorating his mother's kitchen walls with finger paints. His mother then enrolled him in an art class in elementary school and the artist bug bit him. He went on discovering his dreams at ASU. His teachers always remarked on his vivid imagination, his own technique, how well he used the tools in his gentle hands. Edwin started sketching from his memory, a picture of Cordelia. He wanted to replace the one that was burned. He realized it was a difficult task to take on, but he wanted to honor her memory. Her face was quickly escaping from his mind.

With her birthday earrings, Rusty noticed she looked like her mom. Even Daniel noticed as Rusty was getting ready. "Who is taking you out tonight Rusty, your team?" he asked.

"No dad, Stan Gertz is." Rusty replied happily. The doorbell rang. Rusty opened it wearing her earrings and her favorite cobalt blue dress. "You look delightful," was Stan's reaction. He extended his hand to Rusty's dad. "Mr. Parker, it's good to see you again."

"Likewise, now you two have fun. Now don't worry about an old man like me," Daniel said with a slight laugh.

Stan drove Rusty to her favorite Italian restaurant, "Amore." Over a bottle of wine, Stan admitted, "Rusty, I have a confession to make. I have had a crush on you since our sandbox days in kindergarten." He was nice not to mention my right-handed sock to his face every time he got too frisky. Stan handed Rusty a small box. "Stan how very sweet," was Rusty's reply. She noticed the pink wrapping paper and smiled. The card attached was equally appealing. Inside she found a ladybug pendant. "Thank you Stan, how perfect," Rusty stated. He helped her put it on and gently kissed her soft check, exclaiming, "Happy Birthday." After they dined, they went for a romantic walk. Stan took Rusty's hand and led her to a park bench overlooking a duck pond. They talked about their future.

Lt. Levitt felt he was getting very close to solving this case. Somebody's future was coming to a curt close. He received an anonymous tip to search Edwin Villa's back yard. Lt. Levitt had a warrant with him as he and his team left to serve it.

"Mr. Villa, we have a warrant to search your back yard," said Lt. Levitt.

"What is this about?" demanded Edwin. As Edwin pulled Rusty aside, he pleaded, "I don't understand."

"I'm sorry. We need to search your home and yard," Rusty said. The caller told them to search the area by the scarecrow. "No stop," Edwin begged.

"Do you have something to hide Mr. Villa?" Lt. Levitt asked. Edwin looked away. He was concerned about them digging in his yard. Since it was an ancient burial ground, he covered the plots with corn stalks and other plants. Edwin didn't dare move the dead because it was considered a bad omen to do so. When he moved to that site he had known of the bodies buried but planted over them anyway. He was concerned that Lt. Levitt and his team would discover his secret. Lt. Levitt motioned for Gavin to start digging. Edwin had a surprised look. There were three markers, which led to three boxes that had been buried. One contained a Tahitian necklace, the other a paring knife, and the third, a picture frame. All three items linked him to Sylvia Crawford's murder. "Edwin Villa you are under arrest." Lt. Levitt handcuffed him as he led him to his squad car.

"I am innocent." Edwin pleaded, "I didn't kill Sylvia Crawford."

"All this evidence we found proves your guilt," Lt. Levitt said. Edwin reflected as he was in the car, he was being framed by the frame that was found.

Gavin wondered, "We have a murder suspect, but who started the fire and why? What do you think Rusty?" Rusty was already out the door.

The case had a strong correlation that kept pestering Rusty. It was the fact that she was seeing her mom who was being misrepresented by Sylvia Crawford. Maybe her mom's ghost was the missing piece to put together this strange case. Perhaps her mom was helping Sylvia through Rusty's visions. Sylvia and Cordelia both knew Edwin. They both would be pleased he was arrested. Though something didn't sit right, something felt very wrong.

Edwin confessed after being interrogated that he started the fire. He explained that he wanted simply to free Sylvia and Cordelia's spirit. He was taken back to his cell, awaiting his arraignment. Arson wasn't dealt lightly in Annabillow; the minimum sentence served was 10-15 years. Edwin still proclaimed he didn't murder Sylvia Crawford.

Rusty's thoughts lingered on the fresh gardenias. They had a correlation too. What did they represent? Gardenias were placed in Sylvia's dead hand. George Radcliff wore a fresh gardenia in his lapel. Edwin Villa grew them wild in his garden. Rusty then remembered hearing from Dorcas that another party had used them too. He had asked Dorcas to put fresh flowers in Sylvia's room daily. Rusty had an idea. She called Lt. Levitt and the team to meet her at the Crawford estate.

"Good Afternoon, Ms. Parker. What may I do for you?" asked Charles.

"My team and I are here to make an arrest, Mr. Morgan," Rusty explained.

"You still think I killed my wife?" asked Charles.

"No but I need to talk to you, your sons, and your staff. May we come in?" Rusty asked. Charles led her and her team into the study.

"Please sit down. I will rally the troops," Charles said. Skyler and River came and sat down next to each other. Dorcas followed Bertha, then Heather. Anges followed Winston. Lauren and Gavin sat down as Rusty noticed the picture of her mom. Lt. Levitt saw her discomfort. At that moment, Stan Gertz walked in explaining, "Your Lt. called it into the media, Rusty. He said the case was about to be blown wide open." I was happy to see Stan but the picture of my mom made me sad.

"Mr. Morgan, why do you have a picture of my mom?" I asked. I realized I was not alone in the room. "The truth Ms. Parker is that at one time

I was in love with your mother. She broke my heart when she married your father," Charles explained.

"I didn't realize you knew her," I said.

"She was Sylvia's art model, but the very first time I saw her was at a dance. Sylvia thought I was too daft to remember. I also was aware they were cousins." Charles began to explain; "Cordelia had a striking beauty, a good heart and a deep soul. Even though she married your dad, I often reflected on the what if's. That picture of her was taken at the dance. It is where I had my first real crush. I have treasured it always."

"Now please take a seat, Ms. Parker. Your team must have something important to state with the media here," Charles said. He saw Brooke Burke with a camera and requested, "No flash photography please." Brooke sat down next to Stan. Lt. Levitt began, "I have gathered you all here at the Crawford estate for a reason. I believe the person who killed Sylvia Crawford is in this very same room." The room fell silent. Suddenly all eyes were on one another. It was an awkward feeling. A rush of warm air passed through me. I have had that feeling before. I knew my mom's spirit was here with me. Stan saw Rusty teeter and quickly came to her aid

before she fell to the floor. Stan took Rusty to the sofa and sat down next to her holding her hand. I was glad he was here. This was the second time Stan saw me faint. The first time was at Sylvia's Will reading.
"I've got your back Rusty," Stan reassured. He had it literally and figuratively.

Lt. Levitt continued, "The killer must have really hated Sylvia to murder her the way he did. George Radcliff was an early suspect but he was exonerated. Edwin Villa was then arrested. Charles Morgan never quite left our thoughts as a suspect."

Charles looked at his sons who seemed distraught by the accusation. "Charles the evidence we discovered shows that you did not kill your wife nor did your sons. The killer is still in this room." Lt. Levitt was waiting for the suspect to come forward voluntarily. "The person who killed Sylvia Crawford is Mr. Anges Reeves," stated Lt. Levitt. All eyes looked directly at him. Anges didn't seem too surprised.

"What?" Skyler said, "You killed my mom?"

Anges came forward in the room and made a statement. He looked towards Stan and said, "I would like to state on record why I killed her."

There was a loud murmuring sound. "Are you sure you want to precede, Mr. Reeves, without a lawyer present?" asked Lt. Levitt.

"Yes, I waive all my rights. I am glad this is finally over. Sylvia can finally rest in peace. I have worked for the Crawfords for a long time, before she married Mr. Morgan. I knew her parents quite well. They were so kind. It was Sylvia who wasn't. She treated all the servants rather badly. When she married Charles, I thought there was hope for her. Maybe he could have redeemed her, but she treated him badly too. She found out a secret about me and was blackmailing me. A long time ago, about twenty-five years back, I had another identity. I was known as Robert Andrews and worked as a butler for another family, the Martins in another town. The lady of the manor, Ms. Melanie, was murdered by my hand. I confessed to the killing and went to jail. When I got out, I changed my name and moved to Annabillow. Braden and Andrea Crawford hired me from an ad I had posted in the newspaper. I continued working at the house even after the Crawford's had died. Years had passed and I was gainfully employed until my profile came up on one of those detective shows Sylvia always watched. She secretly had me investigated and discovered who I really was. She threatened to expose my past if I didn't give in to her demands.

She continuously belittled and humiliated me by making me perform degrading tasks just for her amusement. I needed the job so I gave in until I had enough. I told Charles in confidence what Sylvia was doing and he assured me he would help me. Though as time would tell, Charles was too intimidated by Sylvia to do anything. I just couldn't take it anymore. I had enough! I stabbed her with a small kitchen knife. I made it look like a triangle so the suspicion wouldn't be on me. When George Radcliff was arrested, I thought how perfect, then with Edwin Villa too. But my conscience got the best of me and I had to come clean. I killed Sylvia because I was tired of her bullying Charles and me. She had to be stopped." Lt. Levitt handcuffed Anges and led him to the squad car.

"I thought I was protecting Anges," Charles said as he looked towards River and Skyler. I knew of his guilt but didn't blame him. That's why I had her cremated so quickly. I didn't want anything linked to Anges. I now realize it didn't make any difference since the body had already been examined."

Everyone left the Crawford estate. The show was over. At the station the next day, Rusty asked to speak to Anges alone. She was granted permission and went to the prison. He was waiting across the partition. Rusty sat across from Anges and inquired, "I was wondering how my mom was involved. I kept seeing her; she was helping me with this case Mr. Reeves. Did you know her?"

"Yes, but not very well. Charles had loved your mother very much and often talked about her in private. Your mom was a kind and beautiful woman, Ms. Parker." Anges said.

"How did you manage to set up Edwin Villa? How did you get on his land and why?" asked Rusty.

"I knew that Edwin had given Sylvia art lessons at the lighthouse. I thought he would be an easy mark as a suspect because it was at the lighthouse Sylvia was killed. It just made sense to me. It was easy getting on his land. I went at night, nobody saw me. I saw that scarecrow and it gave me the idea to bury evidence there."

"Do you know who called in the tip to search Edwin's home?" asked Rusty.

"I did. I was trying to put the guilt on him. It took you a long time with this case, Ms. Parker. I thought you were quicker. I left good clues, you think?"

"What about the gardenias?" asked Rusty.

"They were simply your mother's favorite flower," he replied.

"I have one last question, Mr. Reeves. Why did you take the pearls? What was the significance?" asked Rusty.

"Tahiti was a special place to me. Sylvia had travel books that made me linger in deep solitude. I had ventured there with Ms. Martin on several occasions. We had a heartfelt relationship; I was more than just her employee. We were lovers. She never married but had a lot of suitors. One of her lovers gave her a Tahitian necklace. I was planning on buying her the same necklace, saving up every last penny I had. Ms. Martin not only accepted the necklace from this fool, but also his proposal. I was furious. Every time I saw her wear them, it angered my soul. It reminded me that I was just her servant. I rightfully took them back after Ms. Martin passed and kept them with me as a reminder of how I felt about her. Sylvia found the pearls while snooping through my belongings, soon after she found out about my past. She took them and wore them in front of me just to taunt me, knowing I couldn't do anything about it. Charles never questioned her about them. I guess he figured they were a gift from her parents. Sylvia just played along. I knew the truth. I angrily ripped them off her neck after I bludgeoned her."

Anges was taken back to his cell. I want to believe in justice, that it was honorably served today. Even though an accurate arrest was made, I am empty inside because I don't feel my mom anymore. She was with me through Sylvia Crawford during this case. Her spirit guided me down the correct path I needed to take. Even though both women are gone, I want to think they are content with the final conclusion. I left with a new outcome, hope.

Stan Gertz walked into the CSI lab as I returned. "Rusty, I am here to take you out for a celebratory dinner," Stan said. Did I feel victorious? Two women who knew each other well are both dead. I felt I got to know Sylvia better because of this case.

"Stan, I want to call my dad first, but I would love to dine with you." Daniel had heard on the TV about the arrest and asked, "Are you ok Rusty?"

"Yes, I will be home soon dad."

"Are you ready to go?" Stan asked Rusty. For

the first time in a long while, I felt ready. I was ready to close this case, ready to move on with my life and career and most importantly, ready to move on with the man I have loved since kindergarten.

The End?

About The Author

This story came to me while I was on a sailing adventure with my husband Robert and son Seth. We sailed to Catalina in our 32 foot boat. We have sailed there twice now and each time a story emerged as I stood at the helm looking deep into the horizon.

I am a first time writer. I have spent 18 years as an Early Childhood Educator and the last 7 years as a wife and mother. I have found solace in my writing. As in the ocean, I write in waves, as the story flows in and out of my imagination.

Dinah Dillman Kaufman

Printed in the United States
144356LV00002B/7/P

9 781935 105275